Short S

Poetry and

Michael

This edition first published in paperback by
Michael Terence Publishing in 2025
www.mtp.agency

ISBN 9781800949317

Cover design
Michael Terence Publishing

Michael Terence
Publishing

Dedicated to Michael's wife, Shirley,
daughters, Katie and Toni,
grandsons, Mason, Logan and Theodore,
son-in-law, Scott
and brother, Colin.

CONTENTS

MICHAEL RONALD ELDER 1

SHORT STORIES 3
My Guitar 4
Adrian the Accountant - TRUST 6
The Highlander (or Cyril's Last Stand) 10
Glastonbury 2015 No1 12
Betrayal (as I recall) 14
Bag of Chips 19
I'll Always Remember (Loch Ness Monster Model) 21
My Favourite Month (October)
(View from My Conservatory) 23
Sunday Morning Walk Along the Seafront 26
From Bah-Humbug to Mr Christmas 28
The Month of January 29
The Factory – Part 1 – Daytime (noisy) 30
The Factory – Part 2 – End of Day (quiet) 31
Jim the Miner 32
The Who Tickets 33
Photo of Henry at Whitby Abbey 36
Human Cannonball 38
Dad's Know-how Manual (Katie's Frosted-up Car) 40
An Essex Legacy (Weeley 1971) 42
Pat The Tipper-truck Driver 50
Three People in the Same Situation 51

OBSERVATIONS 53
The Clementine 54
The Cushion 55
Ivy Leaf 56
Purple Flower 57

POEMS 59
- **The Icelandic Volcano** 60
- **Tropical Death** 61
- **Breakfast** 62
- **Driver of Our Bus** 63
- **The Decorator** 64
- **Dad's Pride** 65

LIMERICKS 67
- **Mick** 68
- **Daisy** 69
- **Devon** 70
- *For Theodore* 71
- *For Mason* 72
- *For Logan* 73

MICHAEL RONALD ELDER

written before and after his diagnoses of Cancer in 2024

I am a "born and bred" Pitsea man to this day. I was born in a bungalow on St. Michaels Church Hill when Pitsea was very rural and Basildon Town was in its infancy. I attended Pitsea Primary School and then the newly built Chalvedon Comprehensive. I loved participating in sport – especially football and I always had a love of music. My desire at this time was to play the guitar like Jimi Hendrix but my fingers had other ideas. I also enjoyed writing during our English lessons and beyond.

I left school as soon as I could and was offered some good employment opportunities. I thought that my love of music and a penchant for writing could be combined. I got offered a job starting in the mailing room of Melody Maker – the biggest music paper at the time – with the draw of progressing to become a music journalist. This was in Fleet Street and the pay was so low I could not even afford to pay my train fares. This put paid to my creative/journalistic writing.

I became a screen printer locally and moved through other jobs until I trained and became a Factory Production Manager with a national bottling company whilst spending many years (and considerable fees) gaining Industry and business qualifications by attending evening classes. I went on to become Operations Manager / General Manager with a few manufacturing, packaging and distribution companies for around 30 years. Any writing I did during this period was purely business/industry based i.e. reports, British Standards, procedures etc.

I was also involved as a volunteer on a major Essex County Council initiative called Youth at Risk helping young people to realise their potential and this project achieved the High Sherriff of Essex Award. I also became a qualified Disability Equality Trainer and successfully completed a Post Graduate qualification as a Disability Equality Practitioner through Anglia Ruskin University.

This was especially rewarding as I lived with Chronic Pain Syndrome for 37 years.

We celebrated 48 years of marriage to my soulmate Shirley in May 2024. We are fortunate to have two wonderful daughters Katie and Toni and my family life is the best and most important thing in my life. I am also immensely proud to become a grandfather to three lovely boys, Mason, Logan and Theodore. I am very proud to also be a father-in-law to Scott.

I was diagnosed in February 2024 with Terminal metastasized Lung Cancer and was told I only had a few months to live. This devastated me as I enjoyed my life even though in pain, I did not want to leave my soul-mate, children or grandchildren who I love dearly. I have been fortunate to have the life that I have and thank my family for their support through these years.

...completed by Shirley, Mick's wife...

Mick, unfortunately and sadly, lost his battle to cancer on the 23rd August 2024. The legacy he has left was full of love and laughter, hard at times but together we got through it all. The love from myself and his family will carry on and help us through this traumatic and sad time.

He was a man of values and knowing the love he had for us will also carry us through this traumatic time. He will stay alive in our hearts alongside the memories of him, he will never be forgotten.

I hope you enjoy his work as he never felt he was good enough to be published but I feel he should be recognised for his hard work alongside his battle through his pain and traumatic diagnoses.

Mick was someone who had a great presence and you knew he was there; he had friendships that lasted a life time. Once known, you're his friend for life.

I miss him where mere words cannot express and I hope he is out of pain and we will see each other once more.

SHORT STORIES

My Guitar

You sit there majestically, silently reminding me that you are my Master and it has never been the other way around. Your presence oozes beauty that charms my senses of sight, touch and ultimately sound – the wonderful lowing sound that some – like my nemesis John Martyn – can coax gently from you to dance through my ears and waft throughout my soul.

If only I had the same key to unlock your wondrous secret. As in a beautiful view over wondrous countryside – I can only borrow the memory of your melody – it is never mine to keep.

Your wondrous coastline of a shape is so delightful to see and touch – full of smooth curves and turns hewn lovingly from seasoned timber. The rich shades of brown range from light to dark, pale to rich, gold to chocolate as it erupts from the core bathing my eyes with an autumn softness. A strong but perfectly smooth wall of lacquer protects you from harm yet makes it almost compulsory to touch you and feel your gracious splendour.

Rapier like, your long, graceful neck emerges proudly from your body cradling those six taut, sinewy wire strings. This is your body revealing your heart that pulses and perpetuates a life full of wondrous sound when caressed by a loving specialist.

Switches abound around your body to help you sound louder, gentler, longer, better. If only I was as useful to you as the switches. If only I could help you sound better.

I'll just have to settle for being an admiring acquaintance rather than the true love and friend I long to be. I'll just have to admire you from afar whilst drinking in both your strength and power but also the soft flirty messages that drift my way.

You are the Singing Detective in my life – questioning, probing, delving and examining my innermost emotions – waiting to pounce on the slightest hint of a clue I may give away. Then I am guilty as charged of releasing smiles and tears of joy, deep sadness and all emotions sitting in between.

You look so beautifully gracious and innocuous sitting there in your silence just longing to be caressed. Thank you for your unique gift – in the right hands – of immersing my senses and soul in wondrous music.

Adrian the Accountant - TRUST

Adrian Street kicked the door to his boss's office open, aimed his pistol at Belmont's chest and fired three shots. Belmont collapsed instantly, mouth wide open and eyes bulging. At last Adrian had exacted vengeance.

'Adrian are you with us?' came the foggy voice from Anne, the bought ledger clerk. Adrian was back in the room. Another daydream. How many times had he put an end to Belmont now? How long would the festering thought continue? 'Sorry Anne – miles away' he muttered,' back to work'.

Adrian had worked for Packrite since leaving school twenty years ago. It was, and still is, a medium sized packaging and distribution firm. The Company was neither dynamic nor ambitious but steady.

This seemed replicated with Adrian. He had been doggedly working away in the accounts department seemingly unnoticed by most and ignored by others. He had reached the lofty position of Deputy Assistant to the Assistant Financial Accounts Manager – a mealy-mouthed title for a not so prestigious job. His salary was average, being consistently overlooked for an increase. The only upward path would be "dead men's shoes". The one good thing his apparent anonymity had given him was the Company's trust. He needed that.

Adrian was unremarkable in both physical appearance and dress sense - a Marks and Spencer man. His sharp nose and small ears conflicted with his rounder face. He had pale skin with random freckles. He looked as though he needed a closer shave even though it was carried out meticulously every morning. His loose mop of salt and pepper coloured wavy hair were a redeeming feature that he was grateful for. He had a slightly lopsided gait, a legacy from a boyhood accident falling from a tree. His postural deficiencies were compounded by a habitual cracking of his neck. His hands swooped from his shirtsleeves, long and slender as if made for a pianist but the only tune they played was on a calculator and computer keyboard whilst working on symphonies of financial digits.

He lived with Gina, his wife of 12 years, a homely woman and very able Mother to their daughters ten-year-old Alice and Emma now eight. Home was a three bedroomed semi on a small estate where the Sunday front lawn mowing was almost a cult. The family car, a five-year-old Ford Focus, was used daily by Adrian on his ten-mile round trip to work and only ventured further for their annual week's holiday to Norfolk – same week, same caravan.

The only other exception was his monthly trips to Dorset for the Company to audit the accounts of a subsidiary. This four day trip had been going on for ten years. Gina didn't like Adrian going but found it useful in conversations to boost his status. It was that time again. As usual Gina ensured that all of Adrian's packing was done including emergency items such as spare tie in case, he dripped tea on one, plasters in case of a cut, indigestion tablets etc. He didn't complain but often felt like saying 'I'm not going to the Antarctic!'

It was Friday. On Monday it was Adrian's monthly Dorset auditing trip. As usual he was summoned to a meeting with Mr. Belmont the Managing Director to 'touch base' beforehand. He detested Belmont's attempts at business buzzwords copied from Rotary Club lunches, wanting fellow Rotarians to think he was an astute, progressive businessman. In truth he had inherited the company from his father and astute accountancy had kept him prosperous.

At 10a.m. Adrian knocked on Belmont's office door and waited. Everyone had to wait to ensure that staff knew their place and his importance.

'Come' Belmont called and Adrian entered.

'Ah, Adrian' Belmont said, gesticulating to take the chair near the highly polished mahogany desk. Belmont settled himself into his olive-green studded leather captain's chair on the 'important' side of the desk.

'So, bring me up to speed with Dorset Adrian'

'Well, Mr. Belmont' he started 'I am visiting Belpack from Monday and…'

'Management team. Any good?'

'Yes, they have a good production team and…'

'Perhaps we should get rid of some – you know the higher earners. What do you think Adrian?'

'I'm sure that we need them. They are reliable and dedicated. It could be a false economy and…'

'Just thinking. I won't rock the boat but I want it known that we are monitoring them. It doesn't hurt to shake things up once in a while'.

'Yes Sir' replied Adrian. More pointless posturing by the vacuous Belmont. Empty threats to emphasise 'I'm the Boss'.

'O.K. then – I'll touch base with you when you get back' - said every time Adrian went but once out of Belmont's office, he wouldn't even get a 'good morning' until the next time he went to Dorset.

'Yes – err – of course Mr. Belmont. I'll get back to work. Thank you'. He said, appearing grateful. Belmont simply gestured him away with his hand.

Adrian had continued his mild accountant performance.

At 8a.m. prompt on Monday, he said his goodbyes to Gina and his daughters, gave his usual promise of phoning as soon as he arrived, started the Focus and left.

Three hours later Adrian pulled up in the long gravel driveway of a large detached Victorian house surrounded with flowering shrubs and manicured lawns. He opened the boot of the car and took out a different suitcase to the one Gina had packed for him. He walked up the crunching gravel to a large oak front door, delved into his tweed jacket pocket, pulled out two keys and opened the door. Once inside he put down his suitcase. The rumbling noise from the staircase produced a vivacious blonde woman and two young children – just getting used to walking. 'Hello Darling' he said – 'and you two lovelies. I'm so glad to be home'.

Shooting Belmont's wallet was the next best thing to shooting him. Trust has proved a potent weapon!

The Highlander (or Cyril's Last Stand)

Wild West heroes stay with us - like Jesse James and Wyatt
but venture to the Shropshire Hills and you'll meet Alan Hyatt

This is no cowboy plumber (though he may wear a 10-gallon hat?)
for Alan stalks his nemesis who he calls a forest rat

For here in Little Switzerland (or like the Austrian Tyrol)
there lurks an all-day breakfast threat
- in the shape of Cyril the Squirrel

Cyril is not welcome here - there are no ifs or buts
he's hunted down at breakfast time - when he nibbles Alan's nuts

Each breakfast time at Highlands would see Cyril appear
but like a coiled spring Alan pounced and Cyril fled in fear

But Cyril was determined and next day he'd be back
for a bite of Alan's sausage or slice of toast from the rack

We'd watch this chess type feud played out
- like a breakfast time High Noon
with Cyril and Alan both plotting moves to be the victor soon

Then came the day when Cyril knew that he had met his match
He watched in awe as Alan proved that Highlands was HIS patch

A fly came in the kitchen - but now he was quite dead
he hadn't known the lightning speed of Alans crusty bread!

Cyril saw this from afar - it made him feel quite ill
I'd better clear off now (he thought) - or end up on Boot Hill

So, Cyril knew he'd lost and left Highlands for the farms
but then he thought "no - bugger that
- I'll head for Craven Arms!!"

Glastonbury 2015 N01

As Pete Townsend said, in almost ironic tone, on Sunday night prior to a barnstorming Who headline set – "here we are again."

Yes – and how grateful I was for that.

It may seem like "comfy slippers" for an old timer and part of that is true. However, looking through the crowd (on the telly box from my front row recliner chair at home) it was apparent that it wasn't just "My Generation" enjoying the stalwarts of mod rock. A whole myriad of age groups were enjoying this back catalogue even though there was probably nothing on the set list younger than thirty years.

"Music was my first love – and it will be my last" sung John Miles in the seventies. In my case he was spot on.

I still have a spine-tingling moment when recalling the late, great, and unpredictable John Martyn, coming away feeling I'd witnessed the presence of genius.

I watched many talented young acts at Glastonbury including the wondrously compelling Rhodes. I'm not just a "back in our day" man.

So, with an open mind I watched the self-proclaimed "Greatest living rock star on the planet!" Yes, Marmite Man – Kanye West. Well, it's all about opinion.

I tried but the camouflage garb wasn't enough – I could still see him. Worse – I could still hear him too! I know – "how can the 120,000 live audience and phenomenal commercial success be wrong?" Again, it's opinion. It was my musical Ed Miliband moment – curious but would I want to experience it on a regular basis – definitely not.

I've called the wife in from digging latrines in the garden - enhances the festival feel she says (bless her). Glaston BERRY is over.

Pete Townsend can finish for me-

"Hope I die before I get old" – hold on – he bloody never!

Betrayal (as I recall)

"Come on then son, we're off," came the call. I ran from my bedroom and virtually skied down the stairs to put my coat on. It was my ninth birthday and I'd hardly slept all night as excitement gripped me. This was the big present. Dad was taking me to see Spurs. There were few opportunities then to see football on television - just when England played or the Cup Final. I saw Spurs in two consecutive Cup Finals and really liked the name Spurs. It was some time before I realised that Tottenham and Spurs were one and the same.

A loud knock on the front door was answered by Dad. There stood my Uncle Reg – Dad's Brother. "Hello Ron, Happy Birthday young Michael he said – you two ready?"

"Just coming Reg," said Dad. It was some years later that I realised the significance in their names as brothers – another Ronnie and Reggie. I discovered the significance of many things that day.

We boarded Uncle Reg's minibus. I sat next to Dad so no one would separate us. The engine coughed and came to life and away we went.

"We're picking the lads up on the way," boomed Uncle Reg – a big man- a few sizes larger than Dad. He had spent years in ships boiler rooms and his hands were big enough to be used as shovels for the coal. To me he was just a soft and friendly giant.

Soon we stopped for the first time. On came a small man swathed in blue and white scarf and hat. "Hello Big George," boomed Uncle Reg "its young Michael's first time today". A muffled noise wrestled with the scarf and he waved in my direction.

"Dad, I asked, why is he called Big George – he is only little?" "I'll explain later son," said Dad for the first time that day.

Off to the next stop. Who was getting on now? A chunky man with a tight woollen hat that looked borrowed from his little brother. "Climb on Enitay," called Uncle Reg.

"Dad is Enitay Italian?" I asked "No, son," said Dad. "So why is he called Enitay?" I asked. "You'll see son."

The new passenger eagerly found his voice.

"Alright lads. Hello little Michael, your first time ain't it, eh?"

"It's great Ron, - you know - your first game ain't it eh?"

"It's a bit on the old chilly side ain't it eh?"

"If we win today its 3rd place in the table ain't it eh?"

Dad whispered to me - "Now do you see why he is called ENITAY – his real name is Bob but he finishes all his sentences with "ain't it eh". Puzzled I nodded to Dad –he must know what he's talking about.

Next aboard were two men who looked like the same person. I'd never seen identical twins before. "Who are they Dad?" I queried "Oh, that's Doom & Gloom son," Dad replied – adding another "You'll find out later."

As the twins sat down, they called out in harmony "We'll probably lose 4 nil today". Deep groans came from around the other seats and Big George threw a rolled-up piece of paper at them. Everyone was laughing though.

A few stops later and the final passengers were picked up.

By this time, I was thinking "Dad's got a lot of explaining to do today".

The minibus was now buzzing with noise. I then asked the compulsory children's question – "Dad – are we nearly there yet?" Dad smiled, saying the magic words "Yes son – we're here now."

Uncle Reg parked the minibus and announced in his booming voice "All ashore that's going ashore". I let Dad off with this one

– he already had enough explaining to do. There were a mass of coats trying to squash out of the door. "Oi – one at a time shouted Uncle Reg – there's no panic – they won't start without us."

"Yeah – let Ron get little Michael off first – it's his first time aint it eh?" called – Enitay.

Everyone was wishing me a happy Birthday and saying "hope you enjoy it lad", or "you'll bring us luck today".

We got off and started walking down the grimy road. I made sure I was in between Ron and Reg, regularly looking up to make sure Dad was still there.

All around were people – I had never seen so many together.

Wooden stalls lined the road – all covered in blue and white. Spurs scarves, shirts, hats and photos.

"Let's get a bite and go in," said Uncle Reg. We walked on, the air full with the smell of burgers and onions. We stopped abruptly at the end of a long queue. "What's this dad?" I asked. "Burger Bill from Harold Hill," he chuckled "Do you want one son?"

My eyes bulged and my stomach growled. I had never seen such a monster burger and readily accepted Dad's offer. I was fascinated by Burger Bill singing funny little songs about his hamburgers and hot dogs interspersed with shouts of "Hurry up Alfie – the man's waiting" to his harassed assistant before concluding every burger presentation with the chorus of "Any drinks?"

After serious munching I finally finished my burger – the biggest and best of my life. This was before the tide of burger joints around nowadays so it was a real treat. My stomach was now full to bursting point.

The unlikely band of brothers now moved forward with purpose, me striding between Ron and Reg with the rest in formation behind. Everyone seemed to know Uncle Reg as he came to every home game but Dad didn't. I briefly wondered why.

We rounded the bend and there it was. My eyes rose upwards whilst my mouth dropped open. My gaze focussed on a giant cockerel badge on the huge brick wall – just like the one on the Spurs shirt that Uncle Reg and the others were wearing. Strangely Dad didn't have one on. I wondered why but heard him say "Come on Michael – let's go in."

We moved to where there was a man inside a very small room. Uncle Reg handed him tickets and he let us in through a magic gate, one person at a time making a loud clicking noise every time it moved. What a great noise I thought. We were going in the seats above the standing area. The seats were 6 shillings but there was a good view without the pushing and shoving. It seemed a lot of money then. There were nearly 60,000 people inside White Hart Lane that day.

Once through the magic gate Uncle Reg led the way up some steps. There was a rumbling noise that grew louder with each step taken until the sound filled my head – 60,000 people all singing and shouting together. One more step and the mesmeric sight that would stay with me forever opened up. The most wonderful, brightest carpet of green imaginable. The pitch where many of my future hopes would be played out. I was in awe of what was happening and my mouth was open wider than a dentist could hope. I felt such a rush of excitement and my just eaten burger was dancing in my stomach.

I got to my seat as if hypnotised. There was a massive roar – the teams appeared – this is really happening.

I felt a tap on my shoulder and turned round "It's brilliant Michael – a'int it eh," shouted Enitay, followed quickly by "We're going to lose today," dueted by the twins – Doom & Gloom.

And so, it continued for 90 minutes (plus 15 minutes for a half time Bovril) until the final whistle blew with the score Spurs 2 West Bromwich Albion 1 –Magic.

I had become a true Lilywhite and unfortunately it is like a marriage vow – for better or worse, till death us do part.

Well, it has frequently been worse rather than better, but nothing can every replace the magical initiation day – that embedded a lifetime of loyalty into my very soul. I had committed no crime but here I was with a life sentence.

Coming home was a blur with a mixture of singing, laughing and the compulsory "we'll lose next week" from Doom and Gloom.

We arrived home and I excitedly tried to cram the whole day into a garbled, never stopping for breath sentence to my Mum.

Once Dad, Uncle Reg and me were indoors I kept saying "can we go all the time Dad, please, please?"

That was when it happened – like earlier that year when I found out there was no father Christmas.

Uncle Reg and my Mum both said to my dad "you'd better tell him Ron."

My Dad sat me down and said very softly "I have something to tell you son. I can't take you to Spurs all the time."

"But why Dad?" I pleaded.

And then came the knife through the heart.

Dad coughed and then replied, "Because I'm an Arsenal supporter!"

Total BETRAYAL!!!

Bag of Chips

I move back and forth uneasily on the pavement hoping to avoid the conspirators. How many of them are involved in the plot? I really don't know – but it is obvious that their numbers are growing.

As I glance at their H.Q. it becomes apparent that the main activists are still there seemingly plotting together. They must have a recruitment plan to swell their numbers – and it certainly appears to be working. New members flit in and out of the epicentre of intrigue in ever increasing numbers as if bees drawn back to the hive – reporting to the Queen.

They all appear powerless to resist the lure of rewards on offer as they emerge proudly clutching the proceeds of their submission. How can they concede in such a weak and cowardly way? Why don't they have the resolve to fight for freedom from this oppressive regime that has them in the palm of its hand? Why doesn't just one of them say no – enough is enough instead of meekly accepting the "King's Shilling" for joining this army of mercenary greed?

I shuffle past the H.Q. once again – trying to be invisible to those inside. My heart sinks still further as I see even more vulnerable souls entering through another entrance. More being drawn in like moths to a light – not realising that once the light has you where it wants you – well, the rest does not bear thinking about.

The steady stream of these innocents continues entering with grey, long faces and exiting with colourful wide smiles of pride and anticipation whilst all holding packages of reward.

What shall I do? How can I stop them? Where can I find help or reinforcements? Is there a plan that I'm not aware of? I just feel so helpless to stop all of this.

As I ponder all of this a young boy walks purposefully from the exit door and abruptly stops directly in front of me whilst looking over his shoulder for his emerging parents. I look down with a heavy heart and sad expression.

Then I see in the boy's hand the "holy grail" that the army of converts had seemingly sold their souls for. Wonderful light golden shades interspersed with small chocolate brown flecks. Ingot shaped bullion bars with white sparkling crystals scattered amongst them – all laying on neat white paper as if their heads were resting on a soft comfortable pillow. A faint wisp of smoky heat drifts outwards into the cold air. Then a heavenly aroma floats to my nostrils, hypnotising my senses to gang up on my taste buds.

Oh well – I tried. If you can't beat 'em – join 'em.

I'm going to get a bag of chips too!

I'll Always Remember (Loch Ness Monster Model)

Fred is the last surviving full time Loch Ness Monster hunter. After many holidays around the highlands, he felt his mission was to locate and photograph Nessie. In 1991 he sold his house in Dorset, parted from his girlfriend and left his share of a lucrative family business to embark on his mission.

He purchased an old mobile library vehicle for his home and set off. Over the years he stopped to camp in various spots around the loch whilst maintaining his vigil. The library van tired of travelling before Fred and so he parked up at the top end of the loch by the edge of a pub car park with permission of the Dores Inn and has remained there since.

He pays council tax on his dwelling which has no electricity or running water and earns his living making and selling clay Loch Ness Monster caricatures. He has never regretted his decision to become what most would consider kindly to be one of our great British eccentrics. He has found true happiness and contentment – something we all search for but sadly do not all find.

He is a very intelligent man and has helped various people including various well-known celebrities, in the search for Nessie but is totally honest and admits that he has still not seen her.

Meanwhile, we bought one of Fred's Loch Ness Monster models whilst holidaying in the area in 2000. It occupies a place on our mantelpiece and this short poem is testament to the memories it evokes:

A strange creation - made of clay reminder of a holiday spent in wondrous God's country where land and wildlife are so free the awesome peaks and glens so lushall within an inspiring hush Colours merge and blend and flourish the landscape all around to nourish Highland scenes etched on my mind I often reach inside to find Look down the Great Glen to afar across the Loch that looks like tar the strange unease that it evolved – will the mystery ever be solved?

It's made by Fred – the monster spotter who'll remain loch side until he's got her – in his camera safe and sound so he can finally say he's found what this model represents – the Loch Ness Monster – heaven sent.

My Favourite Month (October)
(View from My Conservatory)

Summer has passed and its' warmth, brightness and greenery are sadly missed. However, we have moved into October, a favourite month for my eyes' delight and peaceful mind. I am fortunate to have a grandstand seat for this event - in the conservatory. It faces west and with blinds drawn back acts as the perfect frame for the wonderful images that unfold between it and the horizon. This is my Theatre of Dreams and I have a free ticket.

This afternoon I saw the matinee performance and it did not disappoint. The stars of this particular show were the orchestra of trees and shrubs lining up at the rear of the stage. Different heights, shapes and sizes bonded together by their seemingly well-rehearsed routines as they swayed in the gentle breeze. This was all conducted by the majestic weeping willow to the right of the frame whilst frantically waving its' Bob Marley like dreadlocked branches and their swathes of wild and still green leaves.

The sun broke through on cue to light up the stage and the participants in this story without words. The wonderful range of light to dark brown leaves looking as if cooked lightly through to well done. It was like a wonderfully expensive box of chocolates just waiting for me to make my selection and savour.

Amongst this were randomly positioned raspberry shaded shrubs enjoying their exhausting colour changes as the sun shone over them and then retracted leaving them to have quick costume changes to violets and purples. The centrepiece for this orchestral dance theatre were the stunningly rich and vibrant gold leaves forming a strange yet mesmerising dichotomy - blending in whilst also standing out. Seemingly if heated for too long by the glorious sunbursts they would simply melt and form ingots of solid gold.

These gently shimmering, changing scenes were hypnotic and calming. They needed to tell no story yet their very presence evoked memories mixed with fantasy within my soothed mind. I watch until my friend - the dreadlocked waving willow tree - calmed in the lessening breeze. It is sad to think that in a few short weeks these glorious and vibrant costumes will be cast adrift from the adorned trees leaving them skeletal through winter until spring arrives to re – dress them. With this thought I leave my seat for the intermission.

After an enjoyable meal I re - take my seat in my old but familiar comfy chair back in the conservatory. I decide that playing some music will add to this expected sensory experience and select the One World album by my hero – the late John Martyn.

I am now eagerly awaiting the evening performance. Up until now the vast expanse of sky has taken a back seat supporting role offering a backdrop for others to perform. It is now ready to undertake its' star billing and produce a main event to remember. As I focus on the stage frame it seems apparent that this afternoons' participants have settled and are as expectant as me. It seems that they too want to be in the audience.

I don't have to wait long as the show promptly begins. Above the previous performers – the trees - I look at the sky. It seems to have grown into a vast mesmerising arena that could literally pull you bodily into its' cast as a fairly insignificant extra.

A wonderful, ever moving array of colour and shape. Tramlines of vivid light rake the blue and grey backdrop as if a torch was being beamed very deliberately in search of something lost. Calm blue space is overlaid with dark and light grey streaks of cloud randomly positioned across its background.

Below is a wonderful pink and red glow where the beams of torchlight are fired from. The centre of the glowing mass burns brightly and fierce. It is as a steel furnace waiting to soften the metal it will be fed to bend and shape it by striking with force over an anvil. It is a warm, dazzling sight with a hint of a warning of power and strength.

A long wisp of purple funnels its way upwards like smoke from a fire. It twists and curves its way upwards until it fades into a streak of near white light rushing horizontally across this picture to a destination out of view. Reds, blue, pinks, yellows, whites and various shades in between jostle for star billing position in this ever-moving palette of colour and intrigue.

There are shapes from sharp and jagged slivers of misty cloud to soft marshmallow messages dropped into the unfolding mix of light. Now, like a Neapolitan mix, the view has formed three sections of colour and texture. It ranges from a volatile rapidly changing dark grey top through a bright red static centre to a fading light-yellow base.

It is now slowly merging into darkness as if it is growing tired of performing this beautiful light show for another day.

I feel privileged to have watched in awe at this magical theatre of the unspoken word. No words are needed when this spectacle is capable of sending personalised scripts to all audience members.

I wipe a tear from my eye as darkness draws a curtain on this unrehearsed collaboration of music and rich concerto of colour. This unique combination always reaches inside of me, touches my soul and wrenches buried emotions from their sleep. Thank you, October, for all of your unique delights.

Rest tonight – but please return tomorrow in all of your wondrous colourful splendour.

Sunday Morning Walk Along the Seafront

It is a bitterly cold day but accompanied by the bright sunshine and not a hint of rain – too cold for the airborne water spreader to appear. This is reason enough to forget all normal Sunday rituals such as perusing the sports pages in the newspapers hoping that someone had got it wrong and spurs had won after all. As usual a call to arms was broadcast meaning that we were going out in 5 minutes so get a shift on and be ready. Impulse rules in our house when I feel able to do something.

I put the kettle on to make a quick hot drink before we go whilst Shirley appears- well almost behind a bundle of coats, hats scarves and various other accessories that I am sure Ranulph Fiennes would deem unnecessary for his extreme expeditions. Nevertheless, best to be prepared, eh? After a quick consumed cup of coffee, we were off. "You do fancy going along the seafront don't you?" I ask about a mile down the road. "Yes, that's fine," came the answer I was expecting.

An unusually easy drive later and we were parking up at the Seafront – outside the house I always admired from afar with its wonderful balcony and overlooking the sea – when the tide is in. First, we have the equipment to put on – the aforementioned hats, gloves scarves and coats that made us look like the Michelin man. However, after a few steps closer to the sea wall I am quite grateful that we had them as the wind had a biting chill to it that tried to force its way into our bones.

We started to walk along the seafront, sun shimmering on the full tide, the many varieties of seabirds and well-kept gardens on the opposite side of the road. I think it deserves a far better reputation than it has been labelled with.

As we went along the red tarmac path looking over to the Kent Coast, we came to realise that we weren't the only ones seemingly auditioning for the ice station zebra. Woolen hats and gloves, scarves were in abundance as were Mr Blobby coats, but who cares if you are warm.

We moved along towards the sweet scent of hot donuts and the sight of people enjoying – I think – alfresco dining with an all-day breakfast. This was a really tough task, but we managed somehow to resist temptation.

It was a really pleasant scene with families enjoying the morning together. Small children some with noses running from the cold but still able to devour that ice cream at a rate of knots.

We approached a group of people with their 6 Newfoundland dogs – such beautiful creatures. As I asked an owner if it was ok to stroke the dog a big shake of the head sent a shower of slobber flying in all directions – from the dog and not the owner I hasten to add. With permission from the owner, I vigorously embraced this majestic animal. It felt so good to stroke a real big dog again and it evoked memories of Henry our Old English Sheepdog – sadly long gone.

We sat on a bench looking across at the boats bobbing on the water and felt that O.K. this is not exactly Monaco but Southend has been good for us today.

We went home feeling better for our short excursion.

From Bah-Humbug to Mr Christmas

So here we are in January. It seems strange that it has all gone, the snow, Christmas with all of the festive (and commercial) trimmings and indeed many New Year resolutions that for many disappear as fast as a melting snowman. For a host of people, they have already given up – at least until the next time.

Christmas now seems a strangely enjoyable time. I truly embrace both the genuine and faux reasons for the occasion for the first time in many years. I loved the period as a child and also when my daughters were children but many years of worrying about Christmas annual stocktake in the factory with thousands of commercial product lines. Staff that although for the most part were excellent through the year would decide to give their brains some extra Christmas holiday. Whilst the auditors seemed to get an extra brain as a Christmas present.

It was always a major worry over the period to discover after all the planning and operation we as a company were solvent and indeed made that wonderful journey to profit. That is no longer on my agenda and I must confess that although I frequently miss the buzz of urgency, constant questions, problem solving and plain aggravation I certainly am glad to wave goodbye to Christmas stocktake.

I have suddenly emerged from grumpy old man at Christmas with my bah humbug hat on to become Mr Lets squeeze a few more decorations in here – there are a couple of small gaps.

The Month of January

January, it is called the most depressing month of the year and apparently yesterday the most depressing day. Christmas gone, bills coming in, greyness in the sky and peoples faces and moods.

As I look out of the window everywhere looks stripped of any sparkle. Bare trees – their leaves having left them some time ago, as children leave family homes. The vista appears airbrushed with a shade of gloomy grey with a subtle hint of chilly dampness for good measure. Sunshine and brightness seem both a distant memory and a hope for the future. Not blazing heat as I wouldn't want to miss the springtime. Seasons are the wonderful changeling of this country with the wonderous autumn colours being my favourite.

However, when watching and reading current news it becomes apparent that this visible gloom that I look at from the window would be totally acceptable if it could reverse certain events such as earthquakes and hideous violent crimes that are causing so much human suffering and incredulous disgust. Unfortunately, that cannot happen.

So, it is back to watching people shuffling past the window, wrapped up warm – many giving their first outing to a Christmas present coat or hat. The weather as usual gives everyone a topic of conversation or at the very least a kind of greeting such as "bit chilly aint it" or "looks like more snow on the way".

Still, it is F.A. Cup 4th round day. At least that will cheer me up later when I watch our game on the telly. We are only playing Leeds Utd. So, it's almost like getting a bye straight through to the next round. Never mind – always next year…

The Factory – Part 1

Daytime (noisy)

I turn the key to unlock the chunky but battered wooden door. I enter into expected quietness. After 20 minutes of jangling a collection of keys in search of the right one for each purpose the labyrinth of industry is open and ready for the day's onslaught. After an all too brief period of quiet the steady stream of footsteps is heard entering the premises. Some softly, some click clicking their way towards the clock that rings with recognition of a card being entered into the slot on top to acknowledge each person's arrival. Conversations that are initially heard and understood begin to merge, becoming a background hum as more join the assembly of people. The radio is turned on ready to entertain and inform throughout the day – helping to add light relief to the monotony of the day's activities.

Then the intrusive wail of a klaxon tells everyone in no uncertain terms that it is time to start work. Now the industrial orchestra starts playing with vigour. Machines compete to be crowned the loudest – their massive mix of metal combining to bang, screech, scrape, and scream for attention. Their backing band of hissing compressed air and the initial choir of voices now raise their volume to be heard amongst this cacophony of sound ensemble. Adding to the percussion section is the steady stream of wired metal trolleys being pushed through the area, their different tones determined by the weight and contents of their load. Amidst all of this the radio adds an ever-changing rhythm section and the shrill amplified tone of the phone rings as if adding soprano interludes. Ripping sounding tape guns, boxes being dropped, components thudding on to wooden topped benches all add to the rich wall of sound that will doggedly continue for another nine hours.

Another day in paradise.

The Factory – Part 2

End of Day (quiet)

The siren has long since added its theme tune to the menagerie of noise that has been prevalent all day. This is the most welcome sound of the day and is heard by everyone as they tentatively await its arrival to signal their departure for another day. The radio and machinery are switched off and the doors are locked by reversing the key jangling exercise of early morning. As the space is now empty of people and their vocal and physical contributions finished a peaceful quiet descends. At first it seems like silence after the constant barrage of noise throughout the day, but then new sounds emanate as if to indicate that this is now their time.

Final sighs of air leak from machine pipes as if preparing for rest. Creaks and groans from machines take their turn in making themselves heard, reminiscent of creaking bones weary from a long day's toil. There is a rhythmic ticking of heat plates cooling like a clock giving out a timely message. For the first time birds walking on the roof can be heard without competing for attention with the constant daily din beneath them.

They appear to have put on heavy boots just to emphasize the point. Distant traffic whizzing past outside can faintly be heard. Wooden bench tops relax with the wire framed trolleys for company. They both emit pinging and cracking sounds as if in a debate as to who has done the most work today. Every small sound magnifies but is peaceful and easy to accept after the barrage of a busy day.

A time to savour the peace until tomorrow's onslaught.

Let's go home.

Jim the Miner

Jim is a coal miner form Nottingham. He lives half a mile from the colliery in a block of terraced 3 bedroomed houses. He was born in the house next door 40 years ago when his father was a miner. He is the eldest child and has three brothers and two sisters all of whom still live scattered around the town except his youngest brother who moved to Canada ten years ago.

Jim has been married for 20 years to Maggie. They went to the same secondary school and after many years of skirting around each other they got together. They have three sons, Jim jnr, 18 years old, who is the eldest of their sons and just going to university – unheard of in his dads' days. He will be studying to be a P.E. teacher. The other sons Mark and Thomas are 16 and 15. All of the boys play Rugby league on a Saturday and Jim loves going to watch them with his pal Kev whose son also plays Rugby.

After, it is down to the Dog & Duck to celebrate a win or drown the sorrows of a loss. Jim's wife Kathy normally joins her boys for a drink and enjoys the regular Saturday break from cooking when they pick up a takeaway on the way home. It's a happy household even though Jim feels a bit regretful that he had never made the move away from the pit and mining. He was reasonably content and had his regular band of workmates but was looking at his sons and whilst he really wished them to have good careers outside of traditional mining, part of him also felt a little envious that he hadn't had the same opportunities.

The Who Tickets

Tickets on sale from 9a.m. Friday. That's the statement on the website. Friday arrives and at 8.45a.m. I take my seat for what is bound to be a fruitless quest – obtaining tickets to see the Who at the Royal Albert Hall – the culmination of a weeklong series of concerts to aid the Teenage Cancer Trust.

This could be the final Who concert ever due to Pete Townsend's tinnitus problem. I've seen pretty much all of the other big players over the years but these have always slipped through the net. I know that there are only two of the original four members but they still knock spots off of plenty of the so-called giants around at the moment.

As I key in the telephone booking number I glance at the website screening, as I am attacking on two fronts, only to learn that I am number 18,663 in the queue. This does not exactly fill me with optimism as this could fill the Albert Hall six times over. I try to assure myself that this must be spread over the series of different artist's concerts and not just this one but I know that this is the one that most will be looking for and as I need my wheelchair to attend this further narrows my options.

So, I got started on the quest – phone on – redial – "lines busy" answer – phone off – repeat. After a time, this process builds into a rhythm of its own and could form the basis of a new number for them to perform on the night.

As I continue this ritual my mind drifts back to the very first concert that I ever went to, coincidentally at the Royal Albert Hall. I was 14 years old and school versus live bands was a bit of a no – contest for me. I recall feeling almost sick with excitement as I got ready to go. I suppose it was a good thing as I was meant to be too sick to go to school. As I think of the day, I can feel the tingling feeling that welled up from my stomach and raced around my body as if charged with electricity. My throat was dry and rasping when I spoke and I acquainted myself with the bathroom frequently, sometimes necessary – sometimes not, as I waited nervously to leave and join up with my pals. I remember my chest feeling tight and fit to burst as I became anxious, the clock seemed to have decided to "hang around a bit".

I suddenly became conscious that in the present I was developing texter's thumb in repeatedly trying to get through to the box office. How do my daughters manage to text friends 25 hours a day with only two thumbs? I have to adopt a different style and decide to lay the phone down and use a variety of fingers to carry out my laborious and increasingly fading hope, as I've been at it now for 45 minutes.

My new tactic is now in full swing as my mind wanders back to that very first concert. The gleeful feeling of us all being together on the journey – both physically and musically, the laughter and sense of anticipation. I recall entering the majestic auditorium and being surprised that it seemed smaller than it looks on the telly where I had only seen it hosting the annual remembrance activities. Equally I was totally enthralled by its splendour and felt privileged to be there.

I felt invited rather than a paying audience member. I recalled where we sat with the view of the stage indelibly imprinted in my mind. In my memory archive I can still see the three bands coming on and off the stage and being totally immersed in their rocking offerings. It was so colourful, so loud, so wonderful, and so obviously memorable.

"You're through to the box office – how can I help you?" I am jolted back to the present reality by this voice coming from the phone and have to force my thumb to stop jabbing out its monotonous rhythm or I will lose my long-awaited contact. It's now 10.15a.m. I quickly realise that at least I can now officially be put out of my misery when I'm told that all tickets are gone.

As I ask tentatively for a wheelchair space and one accompanying seat ticket I prepare to say "thanks anyway" and put the phone down. I then feel stunned as I hear "yes – we have those seats in the circle". I ask for this to be repeated and once again confirmed by reciting the words back, still not believing that it was mission accomplished as I promptly confirmed the booking.

Due to my health condition, I never know until the actual day if I am able to go or not – as with any appointment. All I can say is for once my daughters had better not take up residence in the bathroom on that day. Here we go again – the excitement is back.

Photo of Henry at Whitby Abbey

Looking at you evokes so many wonderful fun filled memories. To this day so sadly missed and far from forgotten and yet whenever I look at this image or see you inside my head, I cannot fail to smile at some of the comedic antics you got up to that earnt you the "stupid" label – but in the nicest possible way.

In this photograph you manage to combine so many looks. You sit so proud and upright with an air of distinction. A mass of white and grey hair swirls around your body and stands out against the beautifully aged and rustic stone wall in the background. The shades of browns, yellows, and greys in the bricks look like an autumn collection of colours providing a wonderfully natural backdrop for you to show off in front of.

Your white and grey mass looks so regal as it flows, covering one of your eyes and just allowing a peep through with the other. It is the piece of coal used for a snowman's eye and your hair is as the snow. Wisps of pure white dance above your head as if testing the power of the breeze. Below it is your huge snowball of a head before it blends seamlessly with a body full of strength where the white blends with grey.

Square in the middle of the snowball head is where character bursts out in a mixture of black, brown, and pink. The black is a big, round, wobbly blob of a nose that could have been bought from a joke shop. This is met by a ring of brown fur that appears in a circle around that wonderful nose and your mouth. Circus clowns would make their face up like this but all you did was have a drink and – hey presto – your white turned brown. What a great trick.

As my eyes fall a little further down this brown patch, they are greeted by a pale pink carpet of a tongue hanging, as usual, from a dark mystery of a mouth. This undulating pink platform could be a landing strip for bees – as you found out to your cost when you swallowed one.

I cannot touch you but by looking at you I can feel your mighty yet softly covered frame in my mind. Your looks are a dichotomy of strength and dignity alongside natural comedic talent and a lasting ability to attract love from many as a magnet draws metal.

I never tire of looking at a memory that evokes so much emotion - from sadness through immense laughter to true total love and admiration.

Henry my dog - I wish I could have been as good a friend to you as you were to me.

Thanks for being my true pal.

Human Cannonball

So here we are again. My 19th time in the hospital fairground ride called the MRI scanner. This time a brain scan – or in my case the medical equivalent of "In Search of the Lost Chord". I am presented once again with the now very familiar questionnaire that I have just handed in, having completed it at home prior to the appointment, as requested and have also completed twice last week. It's all about metal in the body and its interference with the scanning procedure so I understand the caution, to a degree, but surely by now they must have deduced that with the amount of metal inside me from surgeries I must be worth more in scrap value than insurance payouts.

I prepare myself by donning the wonderful hospital gown – obviously designed by a committee after a night on the beer with a remit for a garment that cannot possibly be tied up unless by a supremely flexible contortionist. It must also have been a requirement to be of such a style that causes maximum embarrassment and humiliation to the wearer – frantically trying to cover bodily parts best kept private for all parties - whilst being paraded publicly past other waiting patients to the scanner.

After a verbal check of the questionnaire to rival any of Tolstoy's efforts I manage to lay down on the table – dignity now disappearing fast – and moved into the scanner. I follow my usual rituals to avoid claustrophobia as I lay in the tube with my nose virtually touching the inner wall. I close my eyes and imagine various things to distract me from the confine of the tight tube. I think of Spurs winning the Premiership – amazing how ridiculous your thoughts can be when you allow your mind the freedom to roam.

With eyes closed I become more sensitive to other feelings. There is always the wind that seems to blow through the tube – just like being – well, down the London tube really. The recognisable sounds start. The loud intermittent banging as if the Council workforce have arrived with pneumatic drills – and are actually using them. Then quiet spells and the rhythmic chugging sound of a mystery train approaching before the drilling noise resumes. All of the time I am very conscious that I must not move at all or the scan will be ruined. Like all things that you know you mustn't do – like laughing at a funeral – it is inevitable that my nose will itch like never before, but I can't move to scratch it.

The strange hospital smell hangs around, an aroma indefinable but a strange mix of cleaning fluid, antiseptic and hints of substances unknown but not very pleasant. It really is a case of imagining being elsewhere to remain immobile as required. In truth, I don't find it too difficult as I eventually allow my mind to drift and take me to my favourite peaceful meadow by the River Avon where I have spent many happy hours with my family. Time loses credibility and meaning as I drift with photographs in my mind and memories to match.

The noise stops. A voice from a speaker inside the tube tells me the scan is complete. It is not long before I am taken out of the medical tunnel of love.

That's it. Another performance over for the human cannonball.

Dad's Know-how Manual

(Katie's Frosted-up Car)

It's a freezing cold morning. Katie's car has been left uncovered on the road overnight and the windows are caked with ice. She emerges from her house – no earlier than usual and immediately realises that she will be late for work as the ice needs clearing.

As Katie hunts around for a scraper her dad comes out. "Where is your scraper, Katie?" he asks. "I said to make sure you keep it handy." "I can't find it," says Katie as Dad instantly produces one from his coat pocket and hands it to her. She starts to attack the ice on her windscreen with the scraper. It is tough going so she reaches inside her car and pulls out a can of de-icer spray.

Dad re-appears. "No – don't use that Katie - it will smear your windscreen and damage your paintwork," he says. Katie feels flustered but replies "It's O.K. Dad, I'm fine -you go back indoors". Dad obliges as Katie resumes scraping only for him to quickly return offering more pearls of wisdom. "Turn the engine on Katie and then the heater on to the screen". "O.K. Dad," mutters Katie and follows the latest instruction as Dad returns to the house. She pulls the first windscreen wiper from the glass giving an immediate signal for her dad to return with the next instalment of advice. "Katie – be careful or you'll pull the rubber off". "I am," insists Katie – by now feeling a whole lot warmer than the windscreen.

She carries on scraping and with the heat from inside the car now increasing she starts to find it a little easier.

Time for the "return of Dad". Katie waits for the next gem from the "ice scrapers handbook" but Dad merely offers, "Sorry I go on a bit love – I'll keep quiet and just scrape the other windows." Katie laughs and replies, "Best idea yet, Dad – but thanks for another lesson from the dad's how to manual." Dad smiles knowingly and just carries on scraping.

An Essex Legacy

(Weeley 1971)

Back in 1969 Woodstock was a word synonymous with arguably the biggest music event ever staged. Thanks to film, documentaries, audio recording of the event and huge media exposure it remains legendary to this day. There had been other smaller events before in many locations and in this country the Isle of Wight festival started around the same time and in 1970 dear old Glastonbury was born and now receives mass media coverage.

However, in 1971 it was announced in the music press that there was going to be a festival of progressive, rock, underground music (call it what you will) at Weeley in Essex over the August Bank Holiday weekend. This was greeted with great excitement by those of us who spent most of our free time straining to grow our hair to ridiculous lengths whilst buried in musical exploration. One quite important question was "where's Weeley?" Although we were Essex boys, we didn't know that it was near Clacton. It took a while for the news to spread as "Social Media" information in those days meant passing round a copy of the Daily Mirror or such like. The line-up of bands booked to play was impressive - I shall mention some later – and we could not quite believe this was happening in Essex.

My group of friends immediately looked to pool our resources such as savings (non-starter), wages (slightly better), back of the sofa (strangely worked well for some) and, of course, a top up from Mum and Dad (best source of all). So, we all had enough to buy advance tickets for the astronomical price of £1.50 for the whole weekend including camping (we were shrewd as it was £2.00 without advance tickets) plus food & transport. These were the days of Hyde Park concerts being free so this was expensive.

The Weeley festival was apparently initiated by the Clacton Round Table and an experienced promoter who were reputedly persuaded that it would be a successful plan to raise more money for charitable causes than their traditional Donkey Derby and demonstrate that such a gathering could be peaceful and non-violent (not that I could imagine the donkey derby causing riotous behaviour). In any case we were grateful for the opportunity. Sadly, the tickets were so easy to forge and other issues at the event meant that not as much was raised as expected or indeed it warranted.

Friday evening on 27th August 1971 saw us set off on our expedition to Weeley via bus to Shenfield rail station and then by train to the venue site. I remember that wonderful stomach knot of excitement that had been tightening all week getting towards strangulation point as we approached the site. Here we were – part of the peaceful army being mobilised towards our base camp. Although we had no official uniform – after all we were free spirits with a peaceful common goal (to have a great time – very principled!) there were so many jackets, shirts, greatcoats, tents etc. being worn or used that had obviously been bought from the many Army Surplus Stores around at the time. Now as I draw upon some military comparisons here it has, during this time of austerity, made me wonder who in the Government Defence Ministry at the time had over-ordered so much that getting rid of it became a commercial venture. I digress.

We disembarked in the fading light to be welcomed by a host of Police officers including some dog handlers to guide us to the festival site. It felt surreal and although there was a good relationship with the authorities it still felt as if they were expecting behavioural challenges to deal with. It later transpired that they did (not with the majority – but I shall explain later).

We tramped through the fields until we entered the festival village. This was a mixture of tents, marquees, makeshift tarpaulin shelters and the start of the camping areas. We met up with many friends and there was a magical atmosphere of excitement, expectancy (although of what we didn't know), and overall friendship that we were all kindred spirits here for something quite special.

There were hot food catering-mainly burgers and what seemed like plastic sausages, eggs, chips and extremely baked beans. This grew more appealing as the hunger set in over the weekend. I recall that there was also a Goulash being stirred in a dustbin by someone with a reclaimed tree branch. This was being served and appeared to go down well (I don't know if it stayed down though). This seemed to be topped up and lasted all weekend albeit by the time we passed it on the Sunday it now took two people with considerable effort to stir it in the dustbin. We stuck with the plastic sausages which seemed the lesser of two evils (Mum – I miss your cooking).

We then discovered the official site toilet facilities (could have thrown the Goulash straight in here and bypassed the middle man). The male toilets consisted of a few wooden poles holding up some tarpaulins like a fence supposedly to screen the users from the rest of the site. I'm not sure who they benefitted most. Once inside the screen we were greeted by a very long 10ft. deep trench with strategically positioned scaffold poles designed (I use that word very loosely) to be used as seats. The screens were not very high so those outside could see the heads of people brave (or desperate) enough to attempt using this "luxury" facility and looked from the outside like part of a Punch & Judy show.

I do recall that one poor soul fell into the trench on the Saturday and was finding that although goodwill was the message of the festival - when it came to offering some hands to help pull him out goodwill had gone walkabout (Glastonbury toilets nowadays – "don't know they're born!"). No more on this subject – it should just suffice to say that through preference it was not just bears active in the woods. Washing during the weekend was not compulsory but standpipes to collect cold water were another luxury item available for our open air en-suites.

My mate Mick and me (Mick) - please keep up – were known as the Pitsea Micks (no explanation offered here). We had taken a two-man hike tent lent to us by my dad who had been a Scout Leader for many years and a soldier prior to that. What he had not lent us was the ability to erect a tent properly. On the Friday night we tried pitching up in various locations around the site only to find a better spot and move on.

Finally, we went to the main arena which was not too busy when we got there. We handed our tickets to the nice Hells Angels (who were usually self- appointed "security") and found a good spot fairly central and agreed that we had a fine view of the stage so with just a little help (O.K. –someone put our tent up) we were ready for the start.

The festival got underway at around midnight with a band called Hackensack – a good solid band but not headliners. I don't remember how long they were on stage for but they had to repeat some of their material until other musicians turned up. I fell asleep with The Edgar Broughton Band blasting my ears. The thing with Weeley compared to festivals nowadays (yes-don't know they're born - again!) was that there were so many acts booked that the music only stopped to change bands & equipment – they played right through each night and there was just the one stage.

As I recall we were awoken on Saturday morning by the full volume of Status Quo (quite inconsiderate really – we were trying to sleep). After rousing and enjoying a few bands from our tent it became apparent that we had been joined by many more people. In those days we sat or laid down at open air concerts – none of this standing up malarkey for us. In hindsight photos did look as though we had been evacuated. I recently saw a photo put on a website unbelievably taken just in front of our tent in the arena with me kneeling beside it with a briefcase I had taken for my worldly goods (why did I take a briefcase to a festival? Oh yes – I couldn't find anything else). However, we decided that perhaps our now flattened tent needed re-locating outside of the arena.

As we passed the Festival Village (they were still stirring the goulash) we saw our pal Dennis sitting enjoying the tranquil chanting of the Krishna Temple Monks in their orange garb. He seemed keen to join them so we wished him well, hoped he would like his new haircut and asked if he planned eating his plastic sausages on a plate beside him (he didn't so we did), and moved on.

There was some drama in this camping area as some people – probably even less able at erecting tents than us – had built small tepee type shelters out of the dry straw laying around. The problem arose when they seemed to decide on lighting a cigarette (I think) and admire their construction masterpieces. The blaze spread rapidly but thankfully so did the fire and official security services to extinguish the potential disaster.

I say "official" security services as I have already mentioned that Hells Angels assumed this capacity. Neither faction was a problem to the music fans but apparently there was an almighty battle between these two "security" groups resulting in Angels motorbikes being smashed and injuries sustained on both sides. This did not spoil the intended peaceful nature of the festival though and from what I recall the Police were very good at – well –policing the event. It did seem surreal when arriving home to see front page news portraying a blazing inferno with a bloodbath thrown in (sold papers I suppose).

We finally decided to pitch our tent in the woods some way behind the stage area and this remained base camp until the end. During the Saturday a shout from various sections went up calling for "Wally". This grew into a regular calling from ever growing numbers. Apparently, there are a number of stories linking this to various sources but I think it was simply some people calling a friend. Anyway, over the weekend the calling "Wally from Weeley" became embedded in festival folklore and for long afterwards it would be shouted at many open-air concerts causing a chain reaction throughout the crowds.

Many excellent bands played at Weeley with pretty much an all-British line up. Saturday was spent going in and out of the arena to see various bands, eating more plastic sausages and dozing for a while in preparation for a memorable evening. Barclay James Harvest attempted the tricky task of performing with a full orchestra. This took time to set up and the natives were getting restless. However, it was worth the wait as they concluded a superb set by playing their piece called Mocking Bird. This was against the backdrop of a glorious sunset and as the haunting melodies wafted through the air a large bird landed and stayed sitting on a lone, bare branch of a solitary tree at the side of the stage. This was as if it were staged especially for the performance of Mocking Bird. The band were asked vociferously by the crowd to repeat this song and did (although the bird didn't do overtime and left the tree).

King Crimson were due on next but the running order seemed to change regularly making it a bit of a lucky dip who you were awake to see. I asked Mick to make sure I was shaken awake to see King Crimson but they were so late that I caught a few bars and promptly fell asleep again (not to worry as I caught them the following weekend in Hyde Park for free).

Mott the Hoople appeared sometime during the night and on the back of this and releasing a single they put up the price of seeing them in the Roundhouse Blues Club a few weeks later to an astronomical twelve bob instead of the usual eight or ten (blooming capitalists). For younger readers 12 bob = 60pence.

Our early alarm call on Sunday was the now sadly departed Rory Gallagher. Nobody slept when Rory was on but no one minded either - a great set from a great, much lamented, genuine blues guitar hero. Rory would often turn up at various locations and play his battered, down to bare wood Fender Stratocaster for free. He was revered for being a genuine musician of the people.

We took our sleeping bags and went back to the tent for a while. We passed through the village. There were now two people with a bigger branch stirring the endless dustbin of thickening Goulash (more plastic sausages for us then). There were quite a few of our Basildon crowd of pals and acquaintances now camped in the same area - Dennis being one of them (after deciding that the Krishna Temple orange robes were not his colour perhaps).

The Sunday afternoon brought us a superb set from Lindisfarne with their unique blend of folk/rock with a working-class kick to it. Then it was on to the Sunday evening with a set from the bill toppers – the newly commercially successful T-Rex with Marc Bolan.

The Faces featuring Rod Stewart. Great songs, great performance, great rapport with the audience (including the now statutory kicking footballs into the crowd). This was a truly memorable festival highlight for me and many others.

There were a few acts to follow including the Grease band (minus Joe Cocker), Arthur Brown, and concluded in the early hours of Monday morning with a well-respected club band (still playing with varying line ups today)– Stray.

So that was it. We packed up our tent (and apparently my briefcase) and made our way to the "evacuation" point at the rail station to be packed in the carriages and sent on our way. We had been very fortunate that we had no rain and as a consequence no Glastonbury style mud to deal with.

However, I recall getting home and having the best bath of my life and sleeping the rest of the day (so that we could get down the pub that night and relive it verbally). Mum asked what I would like for dinner. "Anything but sausages or Goulash please," I replied.

Weeley has been referred to as the "forgotten festival". The attendance figures were reported on a scale of 110,000 to 500,000. The truth is probably somewhere in between including those who got stuck in transit. Although the Isle of Wight festival of 1970 had a great line up Weeley was held in very high regard by musicians and music journalists alike and was often referred to as "our Woodstock". It was declared a free festival part of the way through (like Woodstock) because of the huge numbers arriving without tickets.

So, what is the Weeley festival legacy for Essex?

Did it continue for years after? No – never repeated.

Did it lead to the now annual V Festival? Highly unlikely as the times were so different.

I think its legacy lives on in those of us fortunate to be there. No August Bank Holiday goes past without me thinking of it. We continue to carry the memories with us and pass down to younger generations as all good folk tales are with variances over time. This remains whether we live in Essex or only came for Weeley. The legacy for me is an "I was there" statement.

It is sad that there is not more footage and recordings but to me that adds to the mystique.

Oh, and there were some very grateful donkeys at the time who had the Bank Holiday off instead of racing in the Derby.

I just hope that Wally from Weeley is not still there stirring the Goulash.

Pat The Tipper-truck Driver

This seems a bit of a strange one thought Pat. Pat was now driving a tipper truck after years as a deep-sea driver. His catchphrase – which he used relentlessly since his diving days was "up she rises" normally to initial amusement from the recipient changing to "oh no – not again" after the fifth or sixth time of hearing.

Pat's load for today was a tone of farmyard manure and his drop off point was to be the Royal Opera House in London.

However strange it seemed Pat thought to himself – well stranger things happened at sea.

After weaving his way through the busy London Traffic Pat finally arrived at the Royal Opera House. Asking a few people, he was directed to the backstage area where they were frantically involved in scenery moving and costume changes for the performance currently on stage of Swan Lake.

'Can we help you' said the woman who answered the door – "Up she rises," said Pat "I've got a pile of … for you – it will certainly help all your plants grow around your lake…"

Three People in the Same Situation

Katie approached the table and chair clutching her newly acquired book tightly in her left hand. She placed her overfull shoulder bag on the table and the book alongside it. She then positioned the chair where she wanted it and sat down. With a couple of shuffles, she was ready to place the book in a good spot on the table to enable her to read it comfortably.

A quick rummage in her bag produced the red leather case containing her reading glasses – the all-important tool for her mission. A broad smile spread across Katie's face as she opened the case and positioned the glasses in a comfortable position to rest on her nose and ears.

"I am really lucky that they had this book already" thought Katie. She knew it would be so helpful in her studies – which she enjoyed immensely. As she looked down at the prize catch on the table her long blonde hair drooped forward, but not enough to bother her or impede her view of the text she revealed as she turned eagerly to page one. Katie and the book were quickly friends.

Toni hurriedly removed her coat and sat down on the firm chair in the remotest corner of the room. She firmly placed the book on the table in front of her, threw a glance towards the door and checked her watch. She immediately realised that time would not allow her the luxury of reading at a comfortable pace. She had to get the job done and keep the appointment with her friend Sam. They had arranged to meet in the library.

Toni reached into her coat pocket to retrieve her notebook and pen – vital tools in her task of finding references to be used from the book and recording them to re – use in her report.

At first, she started to flick through the pages with her thumb controlling the pace like a brake. Nothing obvious appeared to cause her to stop.

Now a different tactic was used with the index finger on her left hand passing the pages at great speed whilst her right hand sat firmly on the corner of the book, rising and falling rhythmically as it synchronised with the passing of the pages.

Toni stopped flicking abruptly. She had found her first step towards her holy grail. She picked up her pen and began writing eagerly; copying the valuable phrase she had found that could be so useful in her work. "Well," she thought, "that's a start". A glance at her watch brought a wry smile to her face as she realised "I can do this in time"!

Brian opened the thick book of many pages and sighed. It was study time again. He gazed down at the task in front of him with a mournful look on his round face. His mouth drooped at the corners and his eyes glazed over. A redness was developing in his full face, highlighting his silver hair and beard.

The look of resignation was broken by Brian taking a deep breath, throwing a quick glance around the room and then thumbing the book to groundbreaking page one.

"Here we go then" thought Brian, doggedly embarking on his epic literary voyage – as instructed by his tutor. His eyes scanned the tight lines of words on the page. Now came the battle to re – acquaint his eyes with his brain and encourage them to communicate. He stroked his beard as if trying to disturb a dormant nest of inspiration. He scratched his head in various places seemingly searching for a magic button to press that would help him to focus on the task in hand. Sadly, these tactics were not working.

Suddenly Brian jerked his head upright with a bright look in his eyes and a hint of a smile on his now upturned top lip.

"I know – he muttered – I'll do it tomorrow".

OBSERVATIONS

The Clementine

The clementine is round and orange – or is it?

When I look closer the colour is made up from mainly two different shades of orange. The background is lighter with many darker spots covering much of the surface so that on quick inspection it blends into a single colour. Once again, a deeper look reveals the pigmental darker spots are not uniform but are in fact all probably unique in size and shape. Neither is it totally round in shape. It has individual dents and blemishes that make it more of an oval and then a further indentation where the stalk holding it on to the tail.

The outer skin is shiny and reflects the lights. It is smooth in texture and the shape can be altered by applying pressure. The indentations top and bottom help it to stay in one position **on** the table. Therefore it is not round after all as it doesn't roll easily.

Even-though I do not like eating oranges the mere fact that it is now open causes a tingle in my mouth. Just thinking of it causes a citrus type twang around my taste buds. Even now I can taste the kick in the throat, that it would create if I ate it and the juice spurting into my mouth like a fountain when I bite into it.

It is a taste that refreshes but stings the mouth.

The Cushion

At first glance it appears to be just a flat square shape but almost instantly ripples appear towards the four flat edges. When various bumps, dents and other imperfections are more obvious as the three-dimensional effect begins to draw me in. The edges of the square are reinforced and held together with stitching and a zip reveals itself within one of the square sides. The material covering the object is not as plain brown as at first glance. The closer it is the more the grooved texture of the surface become more visible. The grooves are completely evenly spaced.

On touching, the shape is immediately changed as if it is backing away like a nervous animal. Indentations appear around the square as I push it with my finger. It is soft on the surface and inside its covered shell. It struggles to retain its shape whilst being prodded and poked but settles into a shape we both seem to be happy and comfortable with as I rest my arm.

Ivy Leaf

The long thin stalk runs alone – narrowing as it travels towards the passenger it carries. It is tube like and pale green. The tube appears exact and cylindrical but closer examination reveal blemishes, varying measurements and kinks and bends throughout its body. My eyes follow the line as if being directed towards its fading end. Just at its slimmest point a flourish of dark green bursts into view like a parachute rushing from a string as if to say "here I am – look at me". This is the leaf – the passenger being held firmly and safely by the stalk.

The dark green mass is shaped like a hand with pointed fingers. The pale green of the stalk extends into the leaf and then parts – sending strands to the fingers of the leaf. The whole pattern is just like arteries reaching out to the fingers with veins drifting from them carrying lifeblood to its extremities.

The rich green mass undulates like rolling hills in a country scene. Light settles comfortably in the lower curves causing it to shimmer and shine. This is balanced by the darkness of the upper curves almost shielding the brighter low leaf as if to say "I will guard and protect you"

The leaf is smooth to the touch on the surface but quite sharp on its edges for protection I would assume. It is flexible and can alter shape only to return to where it wants to be when it is not being forced in other directions. The underbelly is a paler green and not so shiny almost as if it has been discovered getting ready to go out but has to put the finishing touches. It does not matter as this is "backstage" to the other sides performance.

A last look at the leaf reveals an island with a wonderful coastline. Beauty lives here alongside strength.

Purple Flower

A flower. An explosion of visual delight. Purple – no it's violet – no it's lilac or is it pink? No – it's all of these and more. A collection of different shades merge to form one overall colour at a glance. Soft oval curved petals bounce lightly off of their surface creating shadows and a shine. A core of firm tightness spirals out to a looser, softer, more open curl, all reaching upwards to drink in the light and perpetuate its plethora of shades and colour.

A simple subject to observe and admire. A complex subject to understand and describe with true justice. Never the less, a great contributor to nature's tapestry of colour and vibrant life.

POEMS

The Icelandic Volcano

The Icelandic volcanic eruption has caused major disruption throughout the whole of Europe. Indeed, my own brother-in-law is stuck in Ukraine and running out of funds. The usual arguments are being put forward by anyone who cares to class themselves as part of the 'media' world. Some are forcefully stating that measures taken for safety reasons have been way over the top. In contrast it could be argued that had it been ignored and a major accident occurred then those same commentators would be vociferously condemning the government and its scientific advisors.

As usual I suppose that once all the furore fades it will be solely financial considerations that are thrust forward and the safety aspects shall be downgraded to the equivalent of leaves on the line as opposed to possible catastrophic consequences. What matters most? Peoples lives or company profits. I don't think I really need to think too deep on that. What we get are superficial soundbites for affect until it suits to pursue another angle.

It will all boil down to Government again anyway, if the Media have anything to do with it. At the moment however, the Government are like Marmite men – love them or hate them – they will be around for a while yet.

Tropical Death

A woman from a tropical country was thinking about when she dies. She is rather a large woman with memories and views of her traditional culture.

As the woman projects her thoughts forward, she makes decisions about what should happen following her death. She does not want her funeral to be European but to follow her own cultural traditions with bright clothing, hot weather and celebration of her life. She does not want any misery expressed lightly but her tropical rights adhered to.

Breakfast

The slightly damp freshness of early morning being slowly ripened by the sun. Whilst the cleanliness tingles the body and other senses start to join in.

Comfortable surroundings, relaxed and good mood.

With the aroma of upcoming food, sizzling sausage, crisp bacon, soft eggs and browned toast. Taunting my taste buds with which I like most.

Coffee beans wafting aroma around to turn up tastes volume without any sound.

Ketchup, pepper, butter and other allies are all added to try it for size.

As each piece of this morning cocktail are eaten, I realise that this breakfast just cannot be beaten.

Driver of Our Bus

To the driver of our bus
With problem passengers bothering us
Won't be plain sailing that's for sure
As they keep coming back for more,
Guilt, anxiety and anger, doubt all gang up to scream
And shout
Why don't you just give this up
Or wander off just like the pup
And not come back and try again to deal
With passengers prompting pain.
But then who would have the victory here would
It be us, or that passenger 'fear'?
So, let's persevere, with mindfulness
To try and calm this passenger mess
We have to try for weeks, months or years
As this old bus rattles through the gears
But try we will from waking till bed and then
We can be miles ahead.

The Decorator

I survey the view from the rooms' window
To raise inspiration for my colour project
Nodding, I reassure myself I know
The choices I have made are correct.
A knock at the door so I move to unlock
And in my eagerness swing a leg faster.
Reminding myself of the time on that clock
was the same as Thursday's disaster.
The pot of paint falls and rolls
As I am invited in tandem –
I wish right now with my heart and soul
I was anywhere else – at random.
Another full paint pot decorating the floor
I'll just have to make a confession.
I can't talk my way out of this one for sure

It's time to change my profession

Dad's Pride

To Katie and Toni – the loves of my life
I'm proud you're my daughters and Mum is my wife
I'm sorry my pain has stopped so many things
Like bike rides & camping and pushing the swings
I know I'm unable to do all I should
But I treasure the good things we did when I could.

The proudest moments that I've ever had
Was seeing you born knowing I'm your dad
I've since seen you grumble & moan, laugh and cry
And having your love brings a tear to my eye
I've watched you both blossom as I knew you would
As your mum has taught you what's wholesome and good.
To inherit so much from your mum is a good goal
To be kind, caring and thoughtful in body and soul.

You're both now grown up with your own families and lives to lead and
Your very own small mouths to feed
I wish for you all that you wish for yourself
Happiness, fulfilment, but most of all health.

I love you both more than you'll ever know
Although during bad times it may not always show
One thing to remember if ever you're sad
You both are so special to a very proud dad.

All my love forever

Dad.

LIMERICKS

Mick

There was an old fella called Mick
Who had to do his homework quite quick
He threw some words down and said with a frown
I hope that this does the trick.

Daisy

A cow called Daisy said 'moo'
Fred the horse said 'I can do that too'
If we stay on the farm
It will do us no harm
And it's better than life in the zoo.

Devon

The break I just had in Devon
Could best be described as my heaven
With sunshine and scenes
To remain in my dreams
I wish it were more days than seven.

For Theodore

We went to the shops did Grandad and me

To get some real Hovis and butter for tea.

For Mason

We went on our holidays did Grandad and me
Right in the New Forest and next to the sea.

For Logan

We stayed in at our house did Grandad and me

And I learnt to climb right up on our settee.

Printed in Great Britain
by Amazon

57622152R00047